First Touch

BOOKS BY TEYLA BRANTON

Unbounded Series
The Change
The Cure
The Escape
The Reckoning
The Takeover

Unbounded Novellas
Ava's Revenge
Mortal Brother
Lethal Engagement
Set Ablaze

Colony Six Series
Insight (prequel)
Sketches
Visions
Travels

Imprints Series
First Touch (prequel)
Touch of Rain
On The Hunt
Upstaged
Under Fire
Blinded
Street Smart
Hidden Intent

Other
Times Nine

UNDER THE NAME RACHEL BRANTON

Lily's House Series
House Without Lies
Tell Me No Lies
Hearts Never Lie
Your Eyes Don't Lie
Broken Lies
No Secrets or Lies
Cowboys Can't Lie

Noble Hearts
Royal Quest
Royal Dance

Finding Home Series
Take Me Home
All That I Love
Then I Found You

Other
How Far

Picture Books
I Don't Want To Eat Bugs
I Don't Want to Have Hot Toes

First Touch

TEYLA BRANTON

WHITE
STAR
PRESS

This is a work of fiction, and the views expressed herein are the sole responsibility of the author. Likewise, certain characters, places, and incidents are the product of the author's imagination, and any resemblance to actual persons, living or dead, or actual events or locales, is entirely coincidental.

First Touch (Imprints Book 0)

Published by White Star Press
P.O. Box 353
American Fork, Utah 84003

Printed in the United States of America
ISBN: 978-1-939203-11-3
Year of first printing: 2018

For all my readers who wanted to know how Atumn met Shannon.

Important Note to the Reader

I hope you enjoy this introduction to my *Imprints* series. In the first novels, I referenced Autumn and Shannon's first case together, and readers wanted the story, so here it is! Though this is a shorter story and as such can't contain the intricacies of the rest of the series, it is a complete story with no cliffhangers.

Note that the *Imprints* series is a spin off from *Then I Found You,* a romantic suspense novel I wrote under the name Rachel Branton. Since the *Imprints* series is paranormal and a little grittier than my Rachel Branton books, I've released it under Teyla Branton.

The *Imprint* series can absolutely be read without first reading *Then I Found You.* **It is a separate series.** But if you'd like to know more about how Autumn and Tawnia found each other, please check out that book.

Also, please note that the collapse of the Hawthorne Bridge referred to in the *Imprints* series is based purely on literary license. The bombing occurred nowhere but in my fertile imagination. Enjoy!

Prologue

I would remember the day forever. I knew because I'd lived through it once before. Tonight I'd have to say a final goodbye to Winter Rain, the only father I'd ever known. I wished now that I hadn't called him by his first name, because only the word *father* could describe the loss I now felt.

Friends were already gathering for the all-night vigil in my living room, where we would share stories and talk about his life. There would be plenty for everyone to say. Winter had loved and helped more people in his short sixty-five years of life than many men could have in ten lifetimes. My mother, Summer, had been the same way. The only good thing about the bridge bombing that had stolen Winter's life was that it had also returned him to her.

A home funeral was our tradition, and even though Winter had been under water for nearly a week after the bridge collapse and some of his skin had been torn away, the cold water had preserved him enough that we didn't have to betray his wishes with embalming. Winter lay inside the simple pine box one of his friends had made, one we would use markers to decorate with messages of love. There was a peace in the stillness of his face that strangely comforted me.

My best friend Jake popped his dark head into the kitchen. "I found the markers. And I've made sure we have plenty of dry ice in the coolers if we need to replace the bags around him."

"Good." With a sigh of relief, I shut the kitchen drawer I was searching and followed him out to the living room, where people were gathered.

Tawnia, my twin sister, with whom I'd been reunited only this week, after thirty-two years of separation, looked up from her conversation and gave me a little wave. Her being here was a comfort every bit as large as the loss that carved up my insides until I didn't know if I could ever breathe again.

Jake stopped and I nearly plowed into him. "What about the picture?" he asked, reaching out to steady me.

He meant Winter's favorite picture of Summer. Because though we'd gathered to celebrate Winter's life, Summer had been the only woman he'd ever loved and a huge part of his life. He'd loved her from the first day they'd met, had adored her through twenty years of marriage, had cared for her during a year of cancer, and had been faithful to her for over twenty years since her death. The picture would bring her back, just for the night, to those who had known her and would remember those stories.

"Oh, right. It's still in his bedroom," I told Jake. "I'll go get it. Can you pass out the markers?"

"Sure."

I turned and went into the bedroom Winter had used. Everything was neat and clean, except the bed where I'd been sleeping to feel close to him. Tawnia must have been at work in here. The picture was on the nightstand in the same spot it had adorned for the past two decades. As a young girl, I'd sat on his bed for hours staring at the picture.

I swept it up and stared into my mother's face. I expected to remember the emotions of the sad eleven-year-old I'd been at her passing, emotions that were forever frozen in time. Instead I felt . . .

An ache so large the world couldn't contain it. An ache that would have been impossible to bear but for the love that also rushed in and filled every crevice and pore, pushing out the ache so I could bask in the warm light of pure love. Loving Summer was the best, most perfect thing I had ever done, and though she was gone, she was still in my heart and would be forever.

I reached out and traced the glass covering her face . . .

I gasped. The hands I'd seen in this strange vision weren't mine but Winter's. And the love I felt wasn't that of a girl for her lost mother, but the larger, more encompassing love of a husband who was completely devoted to his wife.

My fingers became suddenly boneless, and I dropped the picture. It fell . . . seemingly both too fast and in slow motion. Down, down, down to the thin throw rug covering the wood floor. The frame hit the carpet and bounced, slamming into the floor with a loud crash. The glass splintered.

I stood there staring, my chest heaving. Frightened yet exhilarated.

"Autumn? You okay?"

I turned to see Tawnia in the doorway, concern on her face.

"Yes, it slipped."

She rushed in, passing me and picking up the picture. "Not a problem. You join your guests. I'll throw away the rest of this glass and clean up the shards. We can still set the picture out in just the frame. I'll get it replaced for you tomorrow."

"But . . ." The words died on my lips as she left the room with the picture.

I'd wanted to touch it again, to feel the love Winter had for Summer. Even with the all-encompassing ache of missing her, it was the most incredible experience. Almost as though he hadn't died, or at least a part of him hadn't.

Or as though, for an instant, I had become him.

"Thank you," I whispered to the empty room.

My eye caught on the small book of poetry my parents had used to recite their favorite verses while exchanging their vows. Some of the people gathering would remember the ceremony, and would like to hear the poems again. I would. As a girl, I'd had them practically memorized. I lifted the book.

And I was happy. So happy. I stared at Winter, knowing today I would pledge my life to him, knowing my future was safe, our love secure. My eyes met his as I began to recite the poem, the one that explained exactly how I felt about him.

The scene skipped backward to one that had occurred only minutes before the first.

I was the luckiest man in the world, standing with my hand linked to that of the most beautiful woman in the world. Words of a poem slipped through my lips as if I'd written the words myself just for her.

I drew in a swift breath. It was them—Winter and Summer. On the day they'd exchanged their vows. It was as if I were there, seeing an event that had taken place ten years before my adoption. I knew the story by heart, of course. Winter had recited his poem and then Summer had followed. I'd seen it in reverse order, but it was as real as if I'd been standing there.

Carefully, I set the book down and began touching more of Winter's belongings. His favorite mug, his lamp, his shoes, the piece of pottery I'd made for him in grade school. On everything he'd loved, I felt him. Sometimes faintly, like a whisper, and sometimes it was more of a shout. I looked out from his eyes, reliving his memories. I was overwhelmed with the sense of him until I almost forgot I existed, except as he saw me—his beloved child, the daughter he loved more than life. I remembered events I'd never experienced. I understood things I could not possibly know.

Whatever was going on here, I didn't question it. I'd felt an invisible cord tying me to Winter and Summer every day of my life—until they died. I'd felt the same tie from the moment I met Tawnia. It was family. Connection. This was like that . . . but stronger.

Tomorrow, I knew we'd drive to the outskirts of town to a plot of earth owned by one of my father's friends, where we'd bury Winter next to Summer. And then it would be over, and life would return to the closest thing to normal I could find without him. Whatever crazy worlds had aligned to give me this intimate glimpse into Winter's life, I was grateful.

I was also dead wrong.

Chapter 1

Two minutes before the cop entered my antiques store, life was good. My best friend, Jake, had bought Winter's Herb Shoppe and was making regular payments that kept the bank off my back, my own business was growing slowly but steadily, and my recently-married sister was six months along with my niece or nephew. And, perhaps best of all, I'd begun helping people with the strange gift that had manifested the day of Winter's funeral.

Psychometry, it was called, the ability to read emotions left on certain objects. In the ten months since Winter's death, I'd gotten past my disbelief, and with the support of Jake and my sister, I'd begun to use it. I had helped unite lovers, resolved disputes between landlords and tenants, found runaway teens, and even helped several mothers know which of their children were telling the truth.

Through it all, Jake and I had grown closer, which made me begin to hope that maybe we could move past this friendship thing we had going on. Maybe. At least it was a possibility.

Life was good.

Then the cop came.

The electronic bell on my door rang as he entered, and I looked up from the solitary customer I was helping and for a moment, I stared. He wasn't tall for a man—only a few inches taller than I was—but he had presence. His strides were powerful and sure, no movement wasted. From the moment he entered, his eyes locked onto mine and didn't let go.

His hair was that color between brown and blond that was darker in the winter and lighter under the summer sun. May meant the color was probably in the midrange. I couldn't tell if the slightly messy hair was purposeful or if he'd been running his hand through it recently. Either could be true because he definitely hadn't taken the time to shave for a few days. The look suited him. On a hot scale of one to ten, he was at least an eleven.

He looked neither right nor left, and the way he disregarded all my antiques told me he wasn't here to buy. Even with his nice slacks and blazer, he didn't look like a salesman or a politician. No, he was either a writer who wanted to rehash the Hawthorne Bridge bombing or a law officer of some kind, one who skirted the clean-shaven face policy.

Every now and again, as a matter of courtesy, a police officer would stop by with news of the bridge rebuilding. The gesture was overkill for me because my brother-in-law was in charge of the reconstruction, but I appreciated that they offered the information to all the victim's families.

I forced my gaze away and returned my elderly customer's credit card. "Thank you. I hope you enjoy the music box."

The woman laughed, clutching her purchase that I'd wrapped in brown paper. "Oh, I will. It'll make a perfect addition to my collection. Please do call me if you find any more that you think I'd like to see."

"Sure thing."

The man had reached the counter and I felt his stare. I deliberately watched my customer half way to the door before turning to find him staring at me with green-blue eyes unlike any I'd ever seen before. One of my own eyes was blue, but his were a wash of brilliant color that seemed to pin me in place. Or maybe it was only the intent way he stared at me, as though he saw all of me and understood me on some core level no one ever had before.

A stare like that definitely meant he expected something. Most cops didn't, so maybe he was a writer after all. If so, I'd send him packing.

"May I help you?" I asked.

Something flickered in his gaze as it wandered over my face, briefly lingering on my hazel right eye. Most people didn't notice my heterochromia the first time I met them, so I'd give him credit for that.

"I hope so," he said. "I'm Detective Shannon Martin, with PPB Homicide." He held up a badge.

"Shannon, huh?" That was different for a man, at least in my circle, especially for a man who looked like he did.

I pretended to study his badge for a moment. PPB meant Portland Police Bureau, and the badge looked legitimate. So, cop it was.

"Homicide?" I asked. Clearly that was the important thing to take from all his words.

"We also investigate assaults, kidnappings, and missing persons. Right now we have a little girl missing, and I'm here at the request of her father. Apparently, he thinks you're a psychic."

There was no missing the derision in his voice.

"Well, I'm *not* psychic," I said with a bland smile that I hoped didn't reveal the pounding of my heart. So far I hadn't used my ability to solve a serious crime, but all at once I wanted to help that little girl. "I only read imprints."

"Imprints?" He arched a brow in a way that might have been called seductive in another environment. Not that I was noticing.

I gave a little shake of my head. "I call them imprints, because it feels like they're emotions imprinted on certain objects. Like a virtual reality program, or something. They're not on everything, though, like you might think. Only on certain objects."

"Oh, of course." Now the derision translated to a noticeable pursing of his lips, as if he held back words he was too polite to say.

I wanted to tell him to get lost, but there was that little girl and her father to think about. "What happened to her?"

The detective snorted. "Isn't that what you're supposed to tell me?"

"It doesn't work that way." I might be glaring at him, but I didn't care.

"If I tell you what happened, you'll be just that more likely to make something up."

That made me laugh. I lifted my hands and took a step back from the counter. "Fine. Don't tell me anything. But if you want my help, you'll need to let me touch the evidence. I can't read what I can't touch. Don't let the door hit you on the way out."

He nodded sharply. "Then you refuse to help."

"Whatever you need to say to make yourself feel better. But you're the one who obviously doesn't want me involved." I turned and started toward my back room that ran the width of my antiques shop, banging my thigh painfully on the tall stool I kept behind the counter for busy days.

I'd made it only a few steps when the bell at my door rang again. Too soon for the detective to be exiting, unless he could fly. I turned to see the detective still lingering near the counter and a burly man coming into the shop.

"Well?" the newcomer asked. "Did she agree to help?"

"No. She's not a psychic," said Detective Martin. "She verified that. But we both knew she wasn't before we came here. You're going to have to trust that we're doing everything we can."

"But my wife knows someone whose kid lied about cutting a hole in their new playpen, and this woman told her who did it." The burly man's eyes went past the detective to focus on me. His hair was too short to be out of place, but his eyes were wild and his clothing askew. Need radiated from him as strongly as any spoken plea. "You're Autumn Rain, right? Can you really read emotions on objects?"

Just like that my annoyance at the detective vanished. I'd go a long way to help this man. "Yes, I can."

"Then please help me. My Alice needs you. She's only ten. Just a baby. We have to find her."

Before I could answer, Detective Martin said, "Please go back to your car, Mr. Craigwell. I know you're desperate, but whatever you've heard, this woman won't bring your daughter back."

"It's been three days," Mr. Craigwell said, tears welling in his eyes. "You have no leads. If it were your daughter, wouldn't you try everything?" His big shoulders convulsed.

The detective looked at me and then back at Mr. Craigwell. I knew he hated what he believed I represented, but he wasn't immune to the father's suffering.

"Okay, Miss Rain," Detective Martin said, turning to me, his voice gruff and angry. "What do you need?"

"How did she go missing?" I said. "I mean, were there any physical objects present? If she was taken from her home or school, I might be able to pick up imprints there."

The father was shaking his head before I'd finished speaking. "No, it was her birthday. We gave her a new bicycle and she was so excited that she left the party and went for a ride around the block. My wife told her to wait, that she had guests, but she wouldn't listen." He rubbed a tear from his cheek. "Can't blame her. She's been wanting this bike for a while. And she was only going around the block. But she didn't come back." His face crumpled and he started to sob.

Detective Martin and I stood there helplessly staring at each other and Mr. Craigwell. Finally, the detective moved toward him, placing a hand on the larger man's back.

The touch seemed to ground Mr. Craigwell, and with a deep gasp, he reined in his emotion. "They found the bicycle, but not her."

"Did you say bicycle?" said another voice.

We all turned to see Jake, coming from the double doors that joined my store with his Herb Shoppe. We covered for each other on slow days and shared two part-time employees, both of whom were over on his side now. Monday afternoons were always slow for me.

I wondered how long he'd been listening. His dark face was framed by even darker dreadlocks, or locs, rather, barely thicker than pencils. He looked both strong and sympathetic. I met him around the counter near the other men, where his arm brushed mine, letting me know he had my back.

"Mr. Craigwell's daughter is missing," I explained. "They found her bicycle."

Jake nodded. "I heard about it on the news. I'm so sorry, Mr. Craigwell."

"Thank you," Mr. Craigwell said. To Detective Martin, he added, "Can we show her the bike?"

The detective sent a searing stare in my direction. "All right."

The reply took too long for politeness, and what he

really meant was "If we must." I wondered why he didn't outright refuse, if he thought I was such a fraud.

"I'll pay you whatever you ask," Mr. Craigwell said. "More if you come right now."

"Autumn never charges to help people," Jake told Mr. Craigwell, "though I encourage those who are satisfied to buy an antique."

"Of course you do." Detective Martin's smirk was all knowing.

Jake took a step toward the detective, the muscles in his chest straining against his snug T-shirt. "Look, do you have a problem? From what I can see, you're the one who walked into this store asking for help, not the other way around."

Detective Martin's hand lifted to his side, where I suspected he kept a gun beneath his blazer. "Take it easy."

I put a hand on Jake's shoulder. "The detective is just doing his job." I went back behind the counter and grabbed my bag, and also my jacket because it was chilly, even for the middle of May. "Jake, if you'll keep an eye on my store?" Regular customers knew they could come in through Jake's shop when mine wasn't open, and new customers could read the sign.

"Maybe I should come with you." Jake was still glaring at the detective.

"I'll be all right." Reading imprints hadn't hurt me yet, though when negative ones were strong, I felt exhausted afterwards.

"We'll have her back within the hour," Detective Martin said.

"You're right, I'm sure." I gave the detective my best smile, which seemed to deflate him a little. I couldn't help adding, "I appreciate your confidence."

His face flushed and he looked ready to tell me exactly where I could stick his confidence, when Mr. Craigwell spoke. "Thank you, Miss Rain. You don't know what this means to me."

I met the man's gaze. "I just hope I'm able to help."

He nodded as we walked out the door together. Jake locked the door behind us, concern on his face. He'd been my best friend even before Winter died, and if he didn't treat me like a little sister, I would have told him by now how I felt about him.

"You come with me, Miss Rain," Detective Martin said. "Mr. Craigwell will follow us in his car."

"Sure." I guess he didn't want me filling Mr. Craigwell's head with nonsense or hitting him up to buy my antiques.

Mr. Craigwell headed for the gray compact sedan next to the curb, while the detective led the way to an unmarked white Mustang. I wondered if he'd put me in the back like a suspect, but he reached for the front passenger door of his vehicle.

And stopped, staring at the ground.

I followed his gaze, only to find him staring at my bare feet that poked out from the bottom of my broomstick dress.

"Did you forget something?" he asked.

"No."

His gaze lifted to mine, and for the first time I saw the hint of a smile. "You sure about that?"

"I'm sure." I wasn't about to justify my lifestyle choice to him. I hadn't worn shoes for most of my thirty-two years, and wasn't going to begin making exceptions now.

"Okay." He opened the door and let me inside.

He waited until we were in traffic to say, "I don't want you upsetting Mr. Craigwell. When we get there, do your thing, but please don't lead him on."

I wanted to choke the man. "I'm not in the habit of leading anyone on."

"I mean it." He took a hand from the steering wheel and pulled a wallet from his inner blazer pocket. Opening the wallet on his leg, he pulled out a hundred-dollar bill and extended it to me. "I'll give you another hundred once you tell him you didn't find anything."

"And if I do find something?"

He snorted. "Right."

I took the bill.

As he gave me another of his smirks, I pushed the button to crack my window and let the bill slip through the opening.

He cursed and slammed on his brakes. "Are you crazy?"

"You apparently think so."

He pulled over and glanced back, as if debating whether or not to go after the bill, which had been run over by several cars before being caught in the wind and vanishing. Too bad because I really did need the money.

He leaned toward me menacingly. "I know your kind, those who prey upon people in need. I swear, I'll put you in jail before I let you take advantage of the Craigwells.

You should take the remaining hundred while you still can. Maybe you can get yourself some shoes."

"You'll have to put me in jail to silence me," I retorted. "If you have nothing to hide, you shouldn't be telling me what to say. Nobody tells me what to say."

"Are you implying that I'm a crooked cop?" His flushed expression was almost comical.

"Hey, you're the one trying to bribe me. If there isn't an imprint on the bicycle. I'll tell him so. And if there's one. I'll tell him that too."

We sat there, gazes locked in a contest of wills that was strangely exhilarating. At least for me. For his part, he was probably thinking of ways to strangle me and toss my body into the Willamette River. Or at least into jail.

I bit my bottom lip, and his eyes dipped, following the motion. No way that could mean what it usually meant when a man looked at me that way. The tension between us increased until I gestured toward the road.

"Well, are we going or not? I'm sure Mr. Craigwell is wondering what happened."

Detective Martin glanced out the back window, noting Mr. Craigwell's car. "Fine." He pulled into traffic.

At least I'd get a chance to help little Alice. I only hoped we weren't too late.

Chapter 2

We rode in silence until I noticed we were approaching the Morrison Bridge. My hands grew moist and my breathing came more rapidly. I knew there were several precincts, and it was just my luck that he was heading to the central one in downtown Portland on the other side of the river.

I still couldn't cross overwater bridges without remembering how it felt being trapped in my car as it plunged into the cold, dark expanse of the Willamette. In fact, I went out of my way not to cross any bridge. It was unavoidable at times, but I could usually prepare myself for it, and even last week, I'd gone downtown with Tawnia after only a few relaxing cups of herbal tea.

I clenched my fists tightly in my lap.

"Are you okay?" Detective Martin's voice had lost its venom.

I nodded, not trusting my voice.

"Oh yeah? Because you don't look okay. Are you having one of your psychic episodes?"

"Just keep your eyes on the road," I snapped.

We were on the bridge now. I kept my gaze locked in front of me, staring at his dashboard and a little slice of sky beyond that. My panic was getting better with every bridge I crossed, so I should thank this arrogant detective for nudging me onto the path of recovery.

"You aren't on something, are you?"

Heat washed over my scalp in a hot flash. "Just shut up until we cross the bridge!" I practically screamed.

He blinked and studied the bridge. He didn't speak for at least a minute and then, "That's right. You were on the Hawthorne when it collapsed. I'm sorry."

I didn't reply. I couldn't. And I didn't care what he thought. As Jake said, it was mind over emotion. I simply needed to concentrate.

I focused on breathing slowly and steadily. My hands relaxed, my heartbeat slowed, and my face cooled. I was in control again. Still, I was glad the detective didn't talk until we reached the precinct.

"Okay, Miss Rain, let's just keep this simple," he said.

At least he didn't offer me another hundred-dollar bill.

Inside, we passed the front reception area, went down a hall, and entered a room full of desks, only half of which were currently occupied by uniformed policemen. We were met by a trim, balding, fifty-something man in a fitted tan suit.

"Hey, Shannon, where you been? You look like something the cat dragged in."

I took a closer look at Detective Martin. Maybe his eyes were a bit bloodshot, but if this was how he looked on a bad day, no wonder he was so confident.

"Miss Rain, this is my partner, Detective Adam Roscoe. Adam, this is the psychic Mr. Craigwell wanted us to bring in."

Detective Roscoe's brows shot up. "Oh, I see." He jerked a nod at me. "Nice to meet you."

"You too," I said, meaning it every bit as much as he did, which was to say not at all. "But I am not a psychic. It's really more of an ability."

Detective Martin pointed to a chair. "Why don't you sit by that desk over there while I get this set up? Please don't touch anything."

"I wouldn't dream of it." I sat in the chair. The desk had to be his, though there weren't any family pictures.

The men withdrew a couple of feet and began talking in low, urgent voices. Several of the other officers at their desks watched them with interest, glancing over at me periodically, so I knew they had to be arguing over me. Patience was never my virtue, so I stood and approached them.

"I get that you want to help the family," Roscoe was saying. "But a psychic? You seriously had to go there? A month until I retire. I don't want to go out on a crazy note. What were you thinking?"

"I cleared it with the chief. She wants the Craigwells to feel we've pursued every avenue."

"Even if it's crap? Jeeze, Shannon. Well, you'll have to do this alone. I'm in the middle of something."

"Did you find a lead?" Detective Martin looked suddenly eager.

"Naw, you were right. The witness didn't pan out. He identified a neighbor's child, not Alice Craigwell."

"Too bad."

I had the sense Detective Martin would have preferred being wrong if it meant bringing Alice home.

"By middle of something, I meant I'm going down to the riverbank with the cadaver dogs."

Detective Martin raked a hand through his hair. "Okay, great, but can you do me a favor first? Mr. Craigwell is probably waiting at the front desk. Can you stay with him or find someone to stay with him until Miss Rain and I look at the bicycle? And don't tell him about the dogs."

"Sure, okay." Roscoe slapped him on the back. "But do you really want to do this? At least we could pass her off to Elvey or one of the rookies. Distance yourself a little."

"No, I'll do it."

"He means he wants to make sure I don't defraud Mr. Craigwell," I said.

The men's heads whipped toward me, their expressions darkening. "I told you to wait at the desk," Detective Martin said.

"I couldn't hear you talk about me over there." I gave him a mocking smile. "Look, I have a business to run. Can we get to this?"

Roscoe laughed and gave me a cheery salute as he backed

away. "Yes, ma'am." To Detective Martin he added, "See you later at the river. Or maybe you should think about getting some sleep."

"I slept last night."

"Two hours on the breakroom couch doesn't count."

Ignoring his partner as he left the room with this parting shot, Detective Martin pulled out his phone and pressed a few buttons before bringing it to his ear. "This is Shannon. I need to get the bicycle from the Alice Craigwell case. Can you have it ready for me? I'll be right there."

He hung up and strode past me to his desk, picking up a manila folder. I hurried after him. As he tucked the folder under his arm, a pen fell out, and instinctively, I bent to pick it up. My fingers touched the pen, and an imprint flashed into my thoughts.

I tapped the pen against my desk as I went over a stack of notes. Pausing, I picked up the picture of little Alice, her white flyaway hair adding a sense of mischief to the bright smile. I had to find her. I couldn't stand to look one more time into her mother's face and tell her I still had no new leads. That I had nothing except the cold fact that her daughter was probably dead.

Before I could experience more, Detective Martin slipped the pen from my grasp. "Thanks," he said, holding it up between us.

I rose to my feet as he did, but I felt disoriented with the partial imprint. I put my hand out to steady myself on the desk before stopping short. Who knew how many criminals had touched that piece of wood?

"You okay?"

I wish he'd stop asking. "Got up too fast, that's all."

His eyes went past me, furrows lining his forehead. "Oh, great," he muttered half under his breath.

I turned to see Mr. Craigwell with a short, red-headed officer, who looked barely out of his teens. We waited until they reached us.

"Roscoe asked me to bring Mr. Craigwell back to wait at my desk," the officer said, his grin disturbing the many freckles on his face. "But he says he's supposed to interview someone with you?"

Detective Martin frowned. "Mr. Craigwell, I think it's better that you wait here with Officer Elvey while Miss Rain looks over the evidence."

Mr. Craigwell shook his head. "I want to be there."

"We'll let you know what happens."

Ignoring the detective, Mr. Craigwell gazed at me, his eyes pleading. "I have to be there, you see that, right? She's my baby. I have to know. Please."

I didn't care if he was in the room, because the imprint would either be there or not, regardless of his presence, but the set of the detective's jaw told me it wasn't open for discussion.

"I know this is horrible for you," I said to Mr. Craigwell. "But the detective is right. I should look at it alone so I can concentrate. But maybe they have a room where you can observe from the outside?" I glanced at Detective Martin as I said this.

He considered for a long moment before nodding.

"Peirce," he said to the red-haired officer, "can you stay with Mr. Craigwell for ten minutes and then bring him down? We won't start until you let us know you're there."

"Sure thing." The young officer's hand shot out to mine, his grin still wide. "I'm Peirce Elvey, by the way, since we haven't been formally introduced."

"Autumn Rain," I said.

"It's a pleasure, Ms. Rain."

His grin was catching. "Just call me Autumn. Ms. is what I call the octogenarian on the second floor of my apartment building."

He chuckled. "Will do. And you can call me Peirce, if you want."

I did want. He was a lot nicer than anyone I'd met so far at the precinct.

"Why not let the father come with us now?" I asked Detective Martin as we left Peirce offering Mr. Craigwell something to drink.

We exited the room and started down a wide hallway. "I still have to grab the evidence. Plus, I wanted to talk to you alone first."

This was getting ridiculous. "Don't worry. I'm not going to lead him on. What do I have to say to make you believe me?"

"It's not that." He stopped in the hallway and waited for another officer to pass us before he continued. "It was nice of you to back me up about not letting him in the room."

I put my hands on my hips and met his earnest gaze. "Look, detective, I don't care if he's in the room. It won't change the imprints. The only reason I said that was to spare his feelings for you, because he has no choice about trusting you with his daughter's life, and I didn't want to make this more complicated. You came to me, even if you don't believe in what I do. That tells me you care about his family, and that you're willing to explore every avenue available to you. That's the only reason I said what I did. Because I feel like you made me lie. And I hate lying."

"Do you now?" He studied me, those brilliant eyes seeming to touch every part of my face. If I didn't know how much he hated me—because of what I did—I'd think he was checking me out.

"Yes."

"Well, Miss Rain, I guess we'll see."

It was on the tip of my tongue to tell him to call me Autumn, but maybe I didn't want to give that favor to a man who so obviously mistrusted me.

He left me alone in a room with four chairs surrounding a table. A short time later he reappeared with a little girl's pink bicycle that was completely covered in clear plastic. "This is the only evidence we have," he told me. "It was found in a park about ten blocks from the child's home."

I stood up from the table and approached the bike. "Isn't that a little far for a ten-year-old to go alone?"

"According to the parents, she's never allowed to go farther than around the block, if that. It's a nice area. Safe. Nothing should have happened to her."

"Yet something did."

He nodded, his face tight. "Of all abducted children

who are murdered, nearly ninety percent are killed and found within the first day."

"Maybe she's not with someone who would hurt her."

"Now that we've ruled out family, that's the hope. But of all stranger or near-stranger abductions, only about sixty percent are recovered."

It was far lower than I'd hoped. "So you're sure it's not a family member?"

"As sure as I can be. All the extended family are close and accounted for." The lines on his face seemed deeper now. "The biggest problem is that three days is a lifetime in a kidnapping. Plenty of time to hide the child—or to hurt them."

Poor little Alice. I touched the bicycle handle through the plastic. A faint imprint of two-day-old frustration reached me—not through the plastic but on the plastic itself. The emotion wasn't strong enough to identify anything about whoever left it.

"I'll need to remove the plastic," I said.

"Shouldn't you sit down? I can bring it over to a chair."

I did usually read imprints sitting down on the stool at my counter, though only a few had been so strong as to require me to sit—the imprint from a woman who left her husband, and another from the backpack of a child who had run away to avoid bullying at school. Those cases had both resolved with happy endings, but this case was far more serious. For the first time, I worried about what I might find on the bicycle and how it would affect me. At my shop, I always kept my parents' book of poetry around in case I felt the need for revitalization, but here I had nothing like that except my four oversized antique rings. They contained faint feel-good imprints, and protected me just a little when I ran across imprints I wasn't expecting, but they wouldn't do much against strong negative emotions.

"Okay." I walked back to the table and pulled out a chair to sit. Then I removed my antique rings and set them on the table, close enough to reach for if I needed them.

Shannon Martin was removing the plastic when Officer Elvey poked his head in the door. "We're out here now, so anytime you want to begin. But the mic isn't on."

"Thanks."

Detective Martin flipped a switch near the door before wheeling the bike over to me. My heart started pounding. What if I found nothing? I wasn't worried about the detective's scorn, but I was worried about the father. I wanted to assuage his grief.

"It's been thoroughly examined for fingerprints," the detective said. "We didn't find any, but I hope that won't interfere with your . . . uh, thing."

"It shouldn't," I said. "Not even washing would make a difference unless it's clothes. Probably because washing destroys the fibers a bit."

"That's interesting." He was watching me intently, and it felt a little too intimate.

Better put this behind me. The handle was the natural place to start, so I reached out and placed my fingers on the one nearest me.

The man jumped out in front of my bike before I even

saw him. Fear shot through me as I slammed on my brakes. He reached for me. My heart pounded. One big hand closed over my arm.

Terror. Mommy! Daddy! Help! He pulled at me. I clung to the bike. I opened my mouth to scream . . . and something filled it. Something soft.

A strong sweet smell made my stomach lurch. I was drowning in it. My hands and arms started to tingle. I was going to die.

His arm went roughly around me. I kicked hard.

Blackness.

Chapter 3

"Miss Rain! Miss Rain!" a voice called from very far away.

I tried to open my eyes, but they wouldn't obey me. My heartbeat was still rapid from the terrifying imprint. Finally, I pulled together the strength to open my eyes.

"What happened?" I asked. Somehow I was on the floor. Or the bottom half of me was. The other half was in Detective Martin's lap.

"You appeared to faint." Skepticism filled the detective's voice.

Was that why he was sitting on the floor holding me? He smelled great and his arms felt safe—until everything came rushing back. The man jumping out in front of me. The terror.

"Oh, dear God," I prayed.

"What?" Detective Martin demanded.

"She was taken. By a man. He had this creepy smile . . .

and dead eyes." My chest convulsed with tears poor Alice hadn't had time to shed. "He stepped in front of her when she was riding her bike on the sidewalk. He held something over her mouth. Something that smelled sweet and strong. It was suffocating."

The detective helped me back up to the chair. "Where was it? Did you notice anything more?"

Tears kept coming as I forced myself to replay the scene in my mind. "She was by a house with a big tree in the front, one with roots above the ground."

"Not at a park?"

"No. There was a car stopped ahead on the road. A pale tan, or off-white. Parked on the wrong side of the street—the right side—with the driver's door next to the sidewalk."

"Is that all?"

"She was so . . ." Belatedly, I remembered her father listening outside the room. I lowered my voice. "Afraid."

"And you're sure that's all?"

Imprints never changed, but sometimes I missed things. And since I'd fainted before the end of it there might be more. I didn't want to touch the bicycle again, but I knew I had to. For Alice.

I must have knocked the bike over because it was on its side. With a shuddering breath, I pushed myself off the chair and knelt beside it on weak knees, grabbing the handle before I could talk myself out of it.

The imprint replayed, the horror every bit as potent as the first time. I tried to notice the houses Alice passed, or anything else that might be a clue, but I could only see what the imprinter saw, and Alice didn't care about houses. Or license plates.

The imprint cut off again as her hands were ripped from the handlebars, but this time I didn't faint. Her limbs were tingling and she was disoriented, but I didn't think she'd lost consciousness at that point.

Another imprint followed from not more than ten minutes before the abduction.

This was the most awesome bike ever! When I got home I was going to kiss my parents and tell them how much I loved it. Super cool. There was my friend Caleb watching me ride by. I straightened my princess crown and waved. He was a nice boy, and I would have invited him to my party if we hadn't been painting fingernails and dressing up. Boys weren't interested in stuff like that. The wind was in my hair, and I reached up to make sure the crown didn't fall off.

That was all. When the abduction imprint began to replay, I pulled back my hand.

"She was wearing her princess crown. She loved the bike, the wind in her face. About ten minutes before the man jump out in front of her, she waved at a friend named Caleb." Tears were still leaking down my face, but I didn't care.

The detective stiffened. "How did you know about the crown?"

Was he an idiot? "There were two imprints. It was in the second, which means earlier. I always see the most recent first."

"Oh, yeah?" He hauled me none-too-gently from the

floor and into the chair. "We didn't tell anyone about the crown. How did you know?" He was practically screaming at me now.

Adrenaline raced through my body, cutting through the weakness left by Alice's last imprint. I jumped to my feet and lifted my chin. Our faces were inches apart. "Because I saw it!"

"Or maybe you're involved!"

"What?" I clenched my fists, which I wanted to ram into him. "Are you crazy? I hadn't even heard of the kidnapping before you walked into my store."

"And why's that? It's been all over the news."

"Which I don't watch! Besides, three days ago I was in Kansas." With Tawnia and Bret, actually, visiting my sister's adoptive parents. "You can check that I was on the flight. But this is insane. Shouldn't you be looking for the guy I saw? Or the tree? Or even talking to her friend? It would make a lot more sense than blaming me."

Whatever else he'd been going to say died on his lips. "You can identify the man?"

"Of course. I saw exactly what Alice saw."

He glared at me for long seconds before saying, "Okay, let's play this your way." He turned to the two-way mirror where presumably Mr. Craigwell and Officer Elvey were watching. "Get me a sketch artist in here pronto!"

I sank back into the chair, my stomach growling and my emotions fragile. I'd do what I could to describe the man and hope they didn't lock me up. One thing about imprints—I could check them any time, so the details wouldn't change.

As long as Alice saw him correctly, we would get an accurate image of the man who'd taken her.

"Stay here," Detective Martin said. "I'll be right back."

Do I have a choice? But I didn't say the words aloud because this wasn't for him, it was for the little girl.

He was probably going to talk to Mr. Craigwell, and I didn't envy him that job. Meanwhile, I had every intention of simply sitting here and recovering. Someone had taken up drumming inside my head, and it took effort to think.

I stared at the bicycle. It hadn't been in a park, which meant some other kid had found it and ridden it there. Or the kidnapper had left it at the park himself. That would mean he'd have to touch it. He hadn't been wearing gloves when he'd grabbed Alice, so maybe he'd left an imprint on another part of the bike. Unlike a necklace or a pair of scissors that could be held in one hand, the bike had numerous parts, and it was conceivable that different imprints might be left on other parts of it. Even if he wiped the bike down to remove his fingerprints later, the imprints would remain.

"Okay, then," I whispered to myself. "If he moved it, where would he touch it?"

I stood over the bike, holding out my hands, considering. Not the handle bars because they would move. No, I'd grab it on the back of the seat and on the short expanse of bar right below the handlebars next to the front reflector.

I touched both places at the same time.

I picked up the bike, walking it over to the open trunk of my sedan. I'd drop this at the park where it would be far enough away that I wouldn't be suspected. With a little luck, it might be stolen, and that would give me more time. It had taken far longer than expected for the chloroform to do its job, but it was easier than the last time without the chloroform. Pretty little thing. I couldn't wait to get her home.

The imprint ended as the man put the bike into the trunk.

I sat abruptly on the hard tile floor, breathing heavily. *It was easier than the last time.* If that meant what I thought it did, Alice wasn't okay, and she might never be okay again.

The door flew open. "What did you see?" Detective Martin was staring down at me, his eyes a mixture of anger and concern.

"It's not the first time," I said. "Alice is the second child he's taken."

Chapter 4

I carefully checked the bicycle for more imprints, without success, and then spent the next two hours with a sketch artist. He helped me create a computer composite before he refined the drawing with an electronic pen directly on his tablet. When he finished, he'd gotten it perfect, from the dead eyes and frightening smile to the dark brown hair and pasty skin. Everything else about the perp was commonplace, from his ordinary looks to his average height and weight. A person no one would look at twice but for those dead, colorless eyes.

I checked the bicycle to be sure I had it right, leaving my finger on the handlebar only long enough to see his face. "It's him," I confirmed.

That must have been Detective Martin's signal to enter the room. He studied the rendering on the screen. "Let's get this out to the tri-county area immediately."

Nodding, the forensic artist grabbed his tablet and left the room.

"Did you find anything about another missing child?" I asked Detective Martin.

"We have several dozen outstanding missing children cases. We're researching all of them to see if there are any similarities to this case."

"It's probably a little girl."

"That's what we think. But then, most children taken by strangers are girls. Look, I'd like you to go with me for a drive around the Craigwells' neighborhood. See if you can locate that tree. There might be evidence in the street, or at least we can start canvassing the area from that point. If he moved the bike as you say, it could have been to protect where he's living."

As you say. I ignored his clear implication that I might be lying.

"We made a drawing of the tree too," I said. "But sure, I'll go with you." Jake would probably be close to closing my shop now. No use in heading back there. "But could we stop someplace and buy something to eat? I didn't have lunch." And all they'd offered me during the long hours I'd been here was a bottle of water.

He blinked. "Oh, right. We have a vending machine."

I sighed. "You know what, I'll wait. I'm sort of a health nut." I preferred to think of it as health conscious, but many people didn't see it that way. Preservatives, GMO foods, and the like were never on my menu.

"We'll rustle something up."

"You sound like you live on a farm."

"Not quite, though I do own an acre on the outskirts of town."

Well that was a surprise. Did that mean he had another life that didn't involve tracking missing persons or solving homicides? I wondered if he owned a dog. Maybe he got his rugged good looks from running around his place and not from working homicide and missing persons.

He led me out of the room and put me at his desk again to twiddle my thumbs. He had a package of salted almonds on the desk, so I opened them and began eating, though they weren't the most healthy version. The jittering feeling inside me eased.

Absently, I rubbed my hand across a basketball-shaped paperweight on the desk. An imprint came to me, at least five years old.

I held the paperweight, surprised at the heaviness of the object. "Congratulations, Shannon," the chief said as she slapped me on the back. "You win most valuable player. Finally, we beat the firefighters." Everyone around us cheered.

"Okay, I'm ready." This from the current-day Shannon, who appeared so stealthily behind me that I almost spilled the almonds.

No, he wasn't Shannon, he was Detective Martin to me, no matter how seeing from his eyes made the separation between friend and acquaintance obsolete.

"What about your partner?"

"He's still with the dogs. This is only a reconnaissance drive. We'll grab something to eat on the way."

"Great," I stood, my finger grazing a notebook on the desk.

Writing a letter to a man named Shannon, a man who'd saved my grandfather's life and who I'd been named after. My family owed him a lot, but what to say to him? He'd been like an uncle to my father, but I hadn't known him all that well. I should make it a point to visit him in England while he was still around. My grandfather would have liked that.

I snatched my hand away. The emotion the detective felt was more for his grandfather than the man he'd been named after, and the strength of it surprised me.

"Something wrong?" Detective Martin asked, his eyes narrowing.

"No." I tossed a few more almonds into my mouth before shoving my hands into my jacket pockets. I wasn't going to touch one more thing in this precinct, if I could help it.

True to his word, we stopped for supposedly organic sandwiches which he, or someone at the precinct, had called ahead and ordered. We ate as he drove, with me downing my entire sandwich before he finished even half of his. The only person I knew who could out eat me was my sister—and that was because she was pregnant.

He chuckled, and I glanced over to see him watching me as we waited at a stoplight. "What?" I asked, lowering the iced tea that he'd also bought with my sandwich.

"You want the rest of mine?"

He probably thought I'd say no. I picked up his second half from the compartment that separated our seats, next to the large silver coffee mug he'd brought from the precinct. "Sure, thanks."

His chuckle deepened. "Glad to be of service." He pulled forward as the light changed. "So how did you get into the imprints business?"

I shrugged. "It just found me."

"How long ago?"

"After the bombing. On the day of Winter's funeral."

"Winter?"

"My father." I stifled my normal urge to share that he'd actually been born Douglas Rayne and that everyone had called him Winter because of his prematurely white hair. When he'd fallen in love with Summer, he'd officially changed his name to Winter Rain. He'd told me it was fate.

"I'm sorry."

"Thanks. What about you? How did you become a detective?"

"My dad was a beat officer. But he's retired now. Lives in Florida with my mother."

"So it's a family thing."

"Not really. He hated it. He did his twenty years and retired to Florida to run a bed and breakfast. It was my grandfather who gave me a love of mystery. He taught history in college for forty-five years, and was a huge Perry Mason buff."

"It's a great old show." I took another bite of sandwich, wanting to ask more questions about his family. Maybe we could even explore that little something that seemed to come alive every time we were together. He had to feel it as strongly as I did.

His next words killed that idea and buried it twenty feet under.

"Look, what you said really upset Mr. Craigwell. You'd better not be yanking us around."

The bite of sandwich turned bitter in my mouth. I set the rest on the napkin in my lap. "Why don't you just take me home?"

"So there isn't any tree." His voice mocked me.

"Oh, there's a tree, and it's going to look exactly like that picture you probably have of it on your phone, but even then, you're not going to believe."

He was quiet a moment. "Okay, let's call a truce. I'll pretend to believe what you say, until I have proof that you're lying."

It was better than nothing. I held out my hand. "You have a deal, Shannon. I can call you that, can't I? Now that we're best buds and all." At some point I was going to call him that aloud anyway, so I might as well give him warning. I might have tried harder to call him Detective Martin, if he didn't insist on treating me like a criminal.

"Do I have a choice?" he asked.

"Not really. I call most everyone by their first name." Which was actually true, so maybe it wasn't only because of his imprints. I'd learned that kind of familiarity from my flower child upbringing with Winter, of course. A little ache began in my gut at that thought because not calling him father was still a huge regret for me. That, and taking him with me that day on the bridge.

His mouth quirked in a brief smile. "We're only about ten more minutes away from where the Craigwells live. I'll let you know when we reach their neighborhood."

"Okay." I continued eating his sandwich, though it had lost its flavor.

We entered a residential neighborhood and had gone several blocks in silence when I started feeling déjà vu. "Stop," I said.

He glanced at the rearview mirror before slamming on the brakes. "What?"

I hopped out of the car, my back facing the way we were going. Shannon climbed out as well and stood staring at me over the car.

"This all looks familiar, but it's backward from Alice's imprint." I pointed across the street. "That's the boy's house. Caleb. From here she turned right."

"So back the way we came."

"Just to the next street. I think she planned to loop around to her house."

"Okay." He disappeared inside the car, and by the time I was back in my seat, he was looking through the file he'd brought with him.

I leaned over when he found what he was looking for: a list of names and addresses.

"Ah," I couldn't help saying. "So she does have a friend named Caleb."

He nodded. "That's the only reason you're here right now."

"Oh, and I thought it was because you had the hots for me." I rolled my eyes as I said it, but was that a little color washing over his face?

"Riiiight. Well, it looks like Caleb does live here."

A little thrill of triumph spread through me, but my smile was brought to a quick halt as Shannon's brows drew more tightly. I bet he was once again thinking I had something to do with Alice's abduction. Sighing internally, I sat back and remained silent.

"This is already a block away from the Craigwells," he said as he turned the car around and followed my directions.

But after turning, nothing looked familiar. I shook my head. "Sorry, there were two imprints. The earlier one was when she saw the boy, and the next didn't start until after the man jumped out in front of her."

Shannon nodded, though I could still see the mistrust in his eyes. "We'll keep going then, like she might have."

Even if she's not what she says she is, she knows something. Much as I hate the idea, she could be involved. I have to follow this to the end. I owe it to Alice.

I yanked my hand away from the silver mug in the console between us, killing the imprint.

Shannon slowed the car, his gaze going briefly to me and then back to the road. "What?"

I held out my wrists. "Why don't you just take me in and lock me up if you think I'm involved. Hook me to a lie detector or torture me. Whatever you need to. You know, normally people thank me for telling them what I see."

"Where is this coming from?" He pulled over to the curb.

"From your stupid coffee mug!" Inside me, anger was building. "Look, it's hard enough seeing what that little girl did, and feeling that pervert's thoughts. I'm trying to help here, and having you glare at me like I'm responsible isn't helping. What more proof do you need?"

I reached out and touched his keys. Those were always great at holding imprints. "So apparently you hate some thin guy in sloppy jeans who comes around the precinct. Enough to want to punch him. Oh, and you really don't want to visit your parents this Christmas." There were other imprints but they were faint. I touched his steering wheel.

My head turned to the woman in the seat next to me. More gorgeous than she realized. And smart and witty. I couldn't seem to tear my gaze away from those unusual eyes. Too bad she was so not my type.

In the imprint, the attraction Shannon felt for me was every bit as strong as what I'd experienced for him when he'd walked into my store. What was wrong with this guy that he could be attracted to someone he so obviously disdained?

"And on this, you're attracted—"

"I get it," he said pulling my hand from his steering wheel. "Look, this is all new for me. I'm doing my best."

"Well, your best stinks." I sat back, folding my arms so I wouldn't touch anything else. "A truce means you keep your suspicions to yourself."

"I thought I had." His words came almost under his breath.

I glanced at his carefully blank face, and despite my anger, laughter threatened to bubble through the chokehold I felt on my neck. He was right. He couldn't help what he imprinted on his mug.

"It's normal to be upset," he said. "This case gets to me too."

Maybe he was right. Maybe it wasn't him or the way he seemed to turn my insides to liquid when he looked at me. No. It was that poor frightened little girl and how helpless I was to protect her.

"Let's go on," I said.

A half block later I saw it: the tree. It loomed on the opposite side on the right, where Alice wouldn't have had to cross the street to ride by it. It wasn't quite as large as it had been from Alice's point-of-view, and the twisted knots were more interesting than scary, but it was definitely a large tree that should be cut down before the exposed roots filled the entire yard. Even now, it had ruined the grass in a large circumference around the tree and bits of missing grass over the rest of the lawn showed more roots surfacing.

Shannon glanced over at me, following my gaze. He pulled to the right curb, a good distance away from the house with the tree.

"It happened closer to the tree," I said.

"I don't want to cover any tire tracks that might be there. Or anything else. Long shot, maybe, but you never know."

"Oh."

We climbed from the car and started up the sidewalk. As we approached the spot where the man had stepped out in front of Alice, I purposefully began replaying the imprint. My breath came faster. Fear crawled over my skin.

I stopped maybe twenty feet from the house with the tree. "Here," I said. My voice was faint. I felt Shannon's gaze on me, but I didn't look in his direction. I was trying to notice anything else that might have been in the imprint.

Nothing. I let it go.

Shannon crouched on the edge of the sidewalk, where he fished something from the gutter with the tip of a pen. He held it up.

A little girl's crown. Alice's crown.

I tried to swallow the lump in my throat.

"Where was his car parked?" Shannon asked.

I walked until I was parallel to the tree. "About here. He must have been following her and passed her to park."

We both stared down into the road, but there were no marks or other features to distinguish this bit of road from any other on the block.

Shannon pulled out his phone, "I need a forensic team at my location. I also need several teams to help me canvass this area. We'll need to visit every house within a two-mile radius. Maybe more. Yeah, I'm sure. Clear it with the chief if you need to. Thanks."

Shannon put the crown in a plastic bag in the trunk of his car, where he also retrieved plastic orange posts and began setting them up in the road from beyond where I said the car had been parked to before where the man had stepped out in front of the girl.

"After three days," he said, "there probably isn't anything to find besides the crown, but I'll let them determine that."

In fact, the street was empty but for a few pieces of trash and faded tire marks. I was doubtful they'd find anything. Shannon had begun tying hazard tape between the posts when the crime scene investigators arrived.

"I want every piece of trash or anything else you find examined," he told them, handing over the crown. "Anything that can help us locate the girl."

Red-headed Peirce Elvey arrived next with six other officers. "Any identification yet on that drawing?" Shannon asked him.

"Nothing in the database," Peirce said. "Maybe someone will see it on the news."

Shannon nodded, glancing at the tree that stood silent sentinel to the scurrying around. "Maybe the neighbors know something." He gestured to the owners of the house with the tree, who had come out on their porch and were staring. The people across the street were doing the same. "Let's start asking. You all have the drawing, right?" The officers nodded and scattered toward the different houses.

"Think they'll find anything?" I asked, remembering a case on the news where a man had joined in a search for a missing child in his neighborhood, only to have police later find the child dead in his basement.

"We can only hope. We've been to a lot of these houses already."

"If he lives anywhere nearby, someone will recognize my composite of him."

Shannon didn't reply, and I wondered if that was him trying to placate me so I wouldn't start yelling again. I didn't plan on it.

"What now?" I asked.

"I'll join the others—after I take you home."

Disappointment shot through me, though that was silly when of course I wouldn't be going door-to-door with him. I started toward the car, and he followed.

"Actually, I would like to talk to that boy sooner rather than later," he said. "He didn't come forward about seeing Alice. If you don't mind waiting for a moment in the car, I'll do it now."

"I'm fine with stopping now, but I don't want to wait in the car. I want to see him."

Shannon stared at me, his expression severe. Not a good look for him. He was going to say no. "Okay," he said, surprising me. "But I do all the talking."

"Thanks," I said, promising nothing.

Chapter 5

Caleb's parents were home, and they were only too happy to call him into their living room to speak with us. The house smelled like roast and fresh rolls, and though I wasn't exactly hungry, it comforted me.

Caleb's round, freckly face paled as his mother explained that we were with the police. He looked the same as in Alice's imprint, though his brown hair was shorter than three days ago.

"Don't worry," Shannon said. "They're easy questions."

Caleb sat down on the couch next to his mother, who wrapped an arm around him.

"So this is about Alice Craigwell," Shannon began. "You know she's missing, right?"

Caleb's head went up and down.

"We suspect that she was taken by a man a little while after she rode by your house on her bicycle. Do you remember seeing her?"

Caleb nodded.

"Was there a car following her?"

The boy's face scrunched up as he tried to remember. "I don't think so."

"She thought of you as one of her greatest friends." The words came from my mouth before I could help them. "She kind of regretted having a girls-only birthday party. She knew you wouldn't want to paint fingernails."

Caleb shook his head. "I like riding bikes, though."

"Was hers cool?" Shannon asked.

This time a head shake. "No. It's pink."

Shannon chuckled. "Right. So did you see which way she went after she passed your house?"

Caleb hesitated, but then shook his head.

"Why did you hesitate when I asked that?" Shannon pressed.

Caleb stared down at his hands. His mother leaned closer to him. "Tell them, honey. It might be important. Did you see which way she went?"

The boy nodded, his eyes fixed on her instead of us. "I thought I did. But when I tried to catch up with her, she wasn't there, so I must have gone the wrong way." He paused before rushing on, "Maybe I could have helped her."

"Oh, no, sweetie." His mom tightened her hold on him. "This isn't your fault."

Shannon was now on the edge of the recliner where he sat, looking ready to fly over the coffee table to demand more. "I want you to think back very carefully. When you followed her, did you see a man parked on the side of the road? He would have been in a light tan car."

Caleb nodded. "There was a man putting something into his trunk. I saw part of a bike tire." The child's eyes widened. "Was that her bike?"

His mother gasped, her hand reaching for her husband's, who sat on her other side.

"We don't know yet," Shannon said. "But did you get a good look at him?" When the boy shrugged, Shannon added, "I'm going to show you a few drawings of people. I want you to look at them and tell me if you see the man, okay?" He pulled up his phone and started tapping. "It'll just take me a moment to set this up."

"So," I asked Caleb while we waited, "did you pass the car, or go back?"

"I passed the car."

"Did the man see you?"

"He nodded and smiled at me, but I just hurried by." Caleb looked far calmer than his parents at this point. They'd probably set new rules for riding his bike now.

Shannon stood and squatted down on the carpet near where Caleb sat. "I'm going to scroll through these images, and you stop me if you see the guy, okay?"

"Okay."

I watched Caleb's face as he studied the drawings, and it changed after the fourth one. Shannon saw it too, and he paused.

"Him," Caleb said. "That's the guy I saw."

Shannon shot me a look, and I knew it was the drawing I'd made with the sketch artist. "Good. Thank you, Caleb."

"Is that the man who took Alice?" Caleb's mother

appeared close to fainting. "I can't believe it. He was that close. What if Caleb—"

Her husband's hand landed on her arm, his head shaking. "Don't go there. You're scaring the boy."

Sure enough, Caleb buried his head into his mother's body and began sobbing. "I didn't know," he said. "They asked us if we saw anything. I didn't know. I thought I turned the wrong way."

"It's okay," Shannon said. "You've helped us now." He arose, extending his phone again to the parents. "What about you? Have either of you seen him around? At school, the store, the park?"

They both shook their heads.

Shannon managed to find a few more questions for Caleb and his parents before I finally said, "Could I see your son's bike?" Maybe Caleb had seen the license plate that hadn't been in any of the other imprints. It wouldn't be the first time an imprinter had forgotten information they had actually witnessed.

A line of puzzlement creased the father's face. "May I ask why?"

The muscle in Shannon's jaw clenched. "Ms. Rain is a consultant with the police department. She is what you might call a sensitive."

At least he'd found another name besides psychic.

The father blinked. "Really? You actually use psychics? I thought that was only on TV."

"We use everything we can to solve crimes, and especially violent crimes. The clock is ticking on this one."

The father nodded. "Yeah. Three days. Not much chance of—" He glanced at his son and fell silent.

We went out to the garage, but the only imprints on the bike had nothing to do with Alice or the man who had taken her. Maybe it was the father's mocking smile that had me say to Caleb, "I think you'd better tell them about the garden gnome. It's the neighborly thing to do."

Caleb's mouth rounded to an O and the mother gave him a hard stare. "What does she mean?" she demanded. "You'd better tell me right now, or you'll be grounded all month from your bike."

She was probably hoping he'd refuse at least until Alice's abductor was captured.

As we walked back to the car, I thought I saw a smile tugging at the corners of Shannon's mouth. "So are you going to explain?" he asked.

"He took his neighbor's gnome in retaliation for not throwing back their ball when they were playing in the yard. Apparently, the man came over to talk to his parents instead."

Shannon shook his head. "Reminds me of how my dad used to yell at kids who crossed our yard to get through to the other block. He wanted privacy without kids popping in at every minute. Now he wishes he'd let them cross because he misses having kids around."

I laughed. "Privacy is something I never had much of until recently. Winter always had some stranger at our apartment. Can't tell you how many months I slept on a mattress in his room so someone could use mine." I missed those times now, and mostly hadn't minded too much, even when I'd been a kid. We had so little when compared with the rich of the world, but we'd had everything that mattered.

"Sounds interesting," Shannon said. "And not quite safe."

I shrugged, unwilling to debate my past with him. He might be starting to believe me, but he wasn't my friend. "You should take me home," I said. I'd driven in to work with Jake today, and he would have gone home by now. "I have to work in the morning."

"Okay." Shannon started the car.

"What about you?" I asked. "Your partner said you hadn't been sleeping for days."

"Plenty of time for that after I find her."

"You can't knock on people's doors all night."

"Yes, I can."

I let him win this one.

When we arrived at my apartment building, I jumped out of the car. "Let me know if you need me to read anything more."

"Okay. Thank you." His formality was back.

"And I'd like to know if you find her."

"I'll let you know."

I shut the door and watched him drive away, experiencing a sad bit of nostalgia for what might have been if we'd met under other circumstances. Less weird circumstances. He seemed man enough to get over my not wearing shoes and eating healthy food, but the hocus pocus stuff meant it was over before it even began. Probably a good thing, since that might interrupt my pining for Jake.

As I unlocked the door to my building and went up the few inside steps to my main floor apartment, I thought about little Alice. Her fear and the slimy thoughts of the man who'd taken her stayed with me, and I didn't know if I'd be able to sleep.

That's why when I opened my door and found Jake there watching TV on my Victorian couch, I nearly shouted in relief. He met me halfway across the room, and I threw myself into his arms.

"That bad, huh?"

I nodded and kept my face buried in his broad chest. He smelled wonderful, like aftershave and a mix of herbs from his shop. I'd be lying if I said he didn't smell a little bit like Winter.

"You want to talk about it?"

"No. I want to eat whatever you brought that is smelling so good and to curl up in Summer's afghan." It was one of the few things I had of my mother that was strongly imbued with her love, and while I tried to use it sparingly in case the imprints would fade or be overwritten by my own, I knew it was going to bed with me tonight.

Jake's expression grew serious. He understood the importance of her afghan, and I knew it took a lot for him not to push me for details. Good thing it was him waiting here instead of my sister, whose vision of being twins didn't include withholding anything for any reason.

He led me to the couch before fishing my parent's book of poetry from his bag. "I was hoping you wouldn't need this, but I brought it from the shop just in case."

"Thank you." I clutched it tightly, welcoming the flood of love from the past. This was one of the reasons he was my best friend, and why I wanted more.

"By the way," he added, "Tawnia called me and wanted you to call her back. Why aren't you answering your phone?"

"I left it at the store." Neither of them could understand why I wasn't glued to my second-hand phone, but they'd stopped teasing me about it. "Text her that I'm fine and that I'll call her tomorrow." I didn't want to call her from my home phone now or she'd hear in my voice that I'd had a rough day and insist on me recounting everything. I'd want to tell her the story eventually, but not tonight.

"Okay, what do you want first, the pot pies from Smokeys, or the chicken wings from Salamander's? I've got them in the oven staying warm."

"Pot pies," I said. "And some of your chamomile tea."

"Already brewing. I'll go get it."

I hugged him again before letting him go. I was lucky to have him, even if he never looked at me as more than a friend. An image of Shannon Martin popped into my head at the thought. Maybe I only liked guys that were unattainable.

I ate my fill of pot pie and chicken wings before I drifted off to sleep during the movie Jake put on. But once Jake was gone and I was in bed, all sleep fled from me, replaced by the images from Alice's imprint. Where was that little girl now?

I held onto my parents' book of poetry, pulled Summer's afghan tighter around me, and willed that Shannon and the other officers would find the dead-eyed man from the imprint.

Chapter 6

The banging on my door started when it was still dark outside. I jolted from an uneasy sleep, cracking one eye to stare at the clock on the nightstand next to my bed. Whoever was banging, it had to be an emergency.

More than one neighbor had awakened me before to ask for some herbal remedy, but less often now than when Winter was alive. He'd been the one with a real talent for herbs and could whip up a sleeping potion or a migraine remedy in less time than it took me to drag my tired body from bed.

"All right, all right, I'm coming," I muttered, though the anxious person behind the door wouldn't be able to hear me. I opened the door without looking through the peep hole.

Shannon stood there, appearing more grizzled than he had when he'd left a few hours earlier. "Don't you even look to see who's out here before you open it?" he said without preamble.

"Don't you know it's barely four in the morning?"

He raked a hand through his hair, and when he responded, it was as though he'd forgotten what we'd been saying. "I need your help."

"What happened?" Belatedly, I realized I was still wearing the clothes he'd dropped me off in, but then he was too, so we were even.

"A neighbor identified your drawing of the perp, and we found the house where he was living."

My heartbeat did a little skip. "You found her?"

He nodded, but his face was grim, his eyes lost. I wanted to hug him.

"She's dead. Three days dead. They found her in one of the rooms on the property. Medical examiner says it looks like she died of chloroform overdose."

"No!" I clutched at the door.

"Her body had been violated post mortem," he added. "We believe the overdose was an accident."

The words from the slime ball's imprint returned to me: *It was easier than the last time.* "He didn't use chloroform the first time."

"That's the thing. You were right about that too. There's evidence of another child—a living child. A girl. But we don't know how much time she's been there or who it might be. Most of the forensic evidence won't be back for days, even rushed."

So not what I'd expected given the television shows I watched. "Which means plenty of time for him to get away."

"We'll get him," Shannon said, his voice choked. "We know his name, Truman Grendel, and we're tracking everything about him. But if he decides to dispose of the evidence . . ."

He'd already killed one child, what was one more?

"What can I do?"

"Come back to the house with me. They're still gathering evidence, but maybe you can find something we won't have to wait for."

I searched his face, wondering if he was really asking for my help, or if he still suspected me and hoped I'd slip and lead him to the man. In the end, it really didn't matter; the result might be the same.

"Okay." Grabbing my jacket and bag, I left with him.

His car was parked illegally in front of my building instead of in the parking lot on the other side. Blue and red lights flashed from his grille and across the front dashboard.

As Shannon started the car, I asked, "Do you have photos of the other missing children?"

"Yeah, they're on a website. Why?"

"If I see a child, it'll probably be through his eyes."

"Right." He took out his phone and brought up the first picture. "Could be any of them really." He handed it to me.

That creep was gonna pay and pay big. If it was the last thing I ever did, I was going to find and kill that sick, perverted, son-of-a—

I dropped the phone into my lap, fished out a pair of thin gloves from my bag, and picked back up the phone.

I had already worked up enough emotion without experiencing Shannon's imprints. I didn't blame him, though.

Shannon winced. "That bad, huh?" For a moment he sounded exactly like Jake.

"Yeah."

"Can you scroll with those gloves?"

"My friend gave me conductive thread to sew into the fingers."

"Smart."

"That would be Jake."

"Guy with the dreadlocks?"

"Locs," I corrected.

Nodding absently, Shannon squealed from the curb, his siren blaring.

I gingerly swiped through the pictures. In each face I saw little Alice as she'd been in the photograph from Shannon's pen imprint—her shy smile, flyaway hair, and blue eyes. It took me a while to get her image from my mind so I could focus on the details of the other missing children. Hard to believe that each of these represented destroyed lives, not just of the child but also those of each family.

"Is there anything that will remove imprints?" Shannon asked. "I have alcohol swabs."

"I haven't found anything that gets rid of them or lessens them except time. Or maybe successive imprints. I've found imprints well over a century old. The newest ones are always first and the most vivid."

"Too bad."

"In this case, it's good for the other child." I hesitated

before asking, "Have you told the Craigwells about their daughter?"

"Not yet. It won't be me this time. My partner went with someone." Guilt tinged his voice.

"Well, I'm glad you came to get me instead."

"I had no choice. I may not believe in what you do, but you gave us the first break we've had on the case."

At least he was honest. I went back to studying the pictures.

When I returned his phone sometime later, Shannon said, "Neighbors never saw a child. And apparently, this guy Grendel works for an online marketing firm. He does all his work remotely. On the side, he remodels houses. He contracts with the owners to live in them for six months or so while he refurbishes them for the cost of the materials and free rent. We don't know much else at this point, but by the time we're finished with him, we'll know everything, including his movie choices and what he eats for dinner. But it'll take time."

Which we didn't have.

"He left the car at the house," Shannon added. "Which was smart now that we've identified it. Must have had another vehicle. Maybe something large enough to tow the car when he moves from place to place."

When we arrived at the house, it was ringed with police cars and personnel. The medical examiner emerged from the house with a gurney supporting a tiny form wrapped in a bag. Again, I recalled the fear poor little Alice had endured. The only comfort, if it was any at all, was that nothing would ever hurt her again. Regardless of what her kidnapper had intended, she'd been saved from his plans.

The officer guarding the entrance recognized Shannon and let him through without looking at his badge. The house looked new inside, which meant Grendel had probably been here awhile. New paint, new carpet, only a few furnishings. One of these was a cheap desk with various black cast-iron organizers that were empty. "Looks like he took all his papers," I said.

"He didn't clear out much more than this desk, which must have held his computer. All the food and dishes and clothing—most everything else still appears to be here. They've been bagging and tagging and taking fingerprints for hours. I was hoping to find some idea of where he was heading, but so far we've come up dry."

I touched one of the organizers and found a brief imprint: *Idiot cops. Just when I was about finished with this place. Well, I've always been one step ahead. Calm. Calm. I dumped all the papers into the box holding the laptop.*

I checked the other organizers and found more of the same: *Ignore the mess. I can organize it again. Just take the most necessary. Don't worry about fingerprints. They'll know who I am now. But plan B will take care of that. I have enough money, so it won't be a problem.*

"These imprints are from after six o'clock last night," I said.

"That would mean he left after we released the drawing you gave us. He must have seen it on the news."

"Probably. He's a neat freak, and he hated throwing all

his papers into the same box. But he's confident he'll be able to stay ahead of you. He has money stashed somewhere."

Shannon snagged a passing man I didn't recognize. "I know you guys have a lot of things you're taking to test, but anything you've cleared, can you give it to us?"

"Sure, this desk is finished, and we've cleared the furniture. There's more stuff in the room where we found the girl."

I began making the rounds, touching things but finding only ordinary imprints that didn't stand out in any way. By the time we reached the room where they'd found Alice, Shannon was beginning to show signs of frustration.

"Furniture and clothing," I said. "And dishes. No one cares much about dishes. He must have taken anything that was important to him. I need something more."

"I'll be right back." He left me near the bed that was stripped of coverings, which had apparently been taken by the forensic team.

A glint of something caught my eye in the mound of clothing that was heaped by the bed, the items somehow not deemed important enough to move to the lab. It was a large shank button, at least an inch across, with a glossy tiger's eye pattern. I knelt down and picked it up, rubbing my thumb across the rounded surface.

I walked on whisper feet into the room, clutching my button in my fist. Poor little girl. She looked like an angel, so peaceful. She would have made a nice little sister. But it was better this way, so he wouldn't hurt her.

I touched her hand with a single finger. So cold.

"I wish it was me," I whispered.

The door opened. "What are you doing in here?"

"Nothing." I closed my hand tightly over the button. I had to be careful not to look into his eyes.

He stepped forward and yanked up my chin. He jabbed a finger at the still little girl. "This is what happens when you don't obey. Remember that."

My body began shaking all over. I couldn't help the tear that rolled down my cheek. Did he kill her because of me? Is that what he meant? What did I do?

"Go clean yourself up." He wrinkled his nose. "You're disgusting."

He was wrong. I bathed this morning when he locked me in the bathroom, right after he brought the still, still girl. He was so angry and had been in there alone with her for a long time. At least that meant he left me alone. He hated to be around me now, and I was glad, but also afraid of what that might mean.

I ran from the room, sliding the hand with my button into my pocket. It was all I had from before, and I had to make sure he didn't see it.

I set the button on the carpet as Shannon returned with a bag of items, and I quickly motioned to him. "I need to see the pictures of the missing kids again."

He knelt next to me and turned on his phone. He started to hand it over, but I shook my head. "You scroll through them."

He started scrolling, and when I saw what I was looking for, I stopped him. "There. Trina Ball. She went missing last year when she was eleven. Last seen wearing off-white jeans and a brown sweater with large tiger eye buttons." I pointed at the button on the carpet. "A girl imprinted on that button three days ago. It was all she had from before, which I assume means before she was taken."

"Three days ago she was alive. You're sure it's her?"

I shook my head. "I haven't seen her face. Just felt what she did. She saw Alice. She wished it was her."

Shannon's jaw clenched. "Try these." He handed me the plastic bag. "They don't seem to have fingerprints that can be used, but they'll be tested for other things if needed, so maybe try to limit exposure."

Not asking if he'd taken the items with permission, I put my hand into the bag. I could feel buzzing imprints coming from a least one object. I rested a finger on the tip of a pen, followed by a business card, and a package of shoelaces. Nothing but a feeling of hurry from the pen. A pair of reading glasses, a bottle of pain killers, and a small notebook also brought no new clues. Next was the remote.

Stupid big oaf of a girl. An image of the child came to mind. No. Not a child. Practically a woman. Her fault all of this. If she hadn't been growing so fast, I wouldn't need another one. It should have been all taken care of with the new girl, but she was unworthy after all. Fragile. Not the miracle I'd first expected when she'd suddenly appeared in my path. That was what I got for deviating from my plans. Well, after I watched a little something to stem my frustration, I'd decide which of the others would take that big oaf's place.

I smiled, thinking of the folder in the car with all the

lovely photos of the lucky girls. Of course, I already knew which one. It should have been her and not the fragile girl in the first place.

At least the chloroform wasn't a complete waste. I knew how I could test it to make sure I got it right for the next time.

Earlier similar imprints followed, where he was upset or angry, blaming it all on "the big oaf" who was definitely Trina Ball and who, at least in Grendel's eyes, did look drastically older than in her "aged" photograph.

"Trina's too old. He wants another girl," I told Shannon, feeling sick to my stomach. "He kept a folder of pictures in his car. Girls he's been watching—did they find anything like that?"

"They haven't started on the car, besides clearing it of anything obvious. But like you said, the guy is a neat freak and there wasn't much there."

"He kept it under his seat in a sort of makeshift shelf. You have to push it in before it will open." Enough pride had gone into thought of the folder's hiding place that he'd probably installed it himself.

"It's worth a try." Shannon was in motion before he'd finished talking. I swept up the button and followed, pocketing it before the entire imprint could replay.

In the garage, Shannon pulled on plastic gloves. He threw open the door to the car, kneeling down to check under the driver's seat. After a few tries, he pulled out a folder, looking hopeful for the first time. He opened it, and we both gasped.

Not one or two photos, but several dozen fell out. I

squatted down next to Shannon, staring at the smiling pictures on the cement floor. All of them were pre-pubescent girls, ten or maybe twelve years old. Each photograph had neatly written details involving the girls' schedules on the back.

"There's not one of Alice," I said. "I mean this picture looks like her, but it's not her." I pointed and Shannon turned the picture over.

"This address is across town. Maybe he removed Alice's picture."

"Or maybe she wasn't planned. He'd thought she was a miracle."

Shannon stared at me. "You didn't say that before."

I swallowed. Great, now I was a suspect again. "Imprints are often feelings . . . it's hard to know what part to explain. I . . . these are the hardest imprints I've ever had to read." Stupid tears clouded my eyes, and I wanted to look away to hide the emotion I knew was in them, but Shannon trapped me with his stare.

He reached out and set a hand on my shoulder. "I'm sorry."

Heat spread through me from his hand, though I hadn't realized until that moment that I was cold. Strange how my heart was breaking for the girls and still somehow had the energy to register a reaction to his touch.

"He's going after her, isn't he?" I said. "But when?"

Shannon's fingers ran down the list of details on the little blond girl's photograph. "Says she starts walking to school with a brother, but they separate a block before the school." Shannon held the picture closer to his face. "It also says the school doesn't call if kids don't come. They just assume the child is sick and send an email the next day. It's up to parents to excuse absences."

"So he'd have all day to get away."

"Not if I get to him first. But my guess is he'll act today. Before we have a chance to sift through the evidence. It would sure help if we knew what he was driving."

"Maybe we can." I stood quickly. "But I'm going to have to touch everything here."

Shannon didn't hesitate. "Do it."

It took thirty minutes, but I finally discovered an imprint Truman Grendel had left on the garage opener near the door. He'd been angry but contained as he'd slapped the opener as he was about to leave.

"Got it," I said, "We're looking for a black van."

Chapter 7

S hannon stood inside the open garage of a house whose owner had let us inside, keeping out of sight, but in position near the wall where he couldn't be seen. Shannon's partner, Detective Roscoe, and two other policemen were likewise hidden along the street in cars that belonged to residents, or in bushes—whatever they could find. The address on the photograph of the girl with the blond hair was next door to where we were now, and our theory was that address marked where the children separated.

I was seated inside a car in the garage, my head resting against the door where no one could see me from outside. But I could see the children as they walked down this hilly street in the direction of the school. We'd been nearly two hours, talking occasionally through the open car window. I wasn't sure if I was here because Shannon worried they wouldn't find Trina with Grendel, or because he wanted to make sure I didn't tip Grendel off. I'd given up caring about anything but trying to help the girl who'd left the button imprint. To save her as we hadn't been able to save Alice Craigwell.

More detectives and officers were targeting other addresses and pictures in Grendel's folder, and part of me hoped he wouldn't show up here, but the other part of me felt it was inevitable. I believe he'd taken Alice when presented with the opportunity because she looked like this girl. Having failed, it was in his organized nature to proceed with his original plan.

Shannon's radio let off a tiny bit of static. "We have eyes on a girl matching the description," said an officer, giving the location.

Seconds later another officer radioed in. "I see her now too. She's with a boy. Should be coming onto the address."

"Any sign of a black van?" Shannon asked.

"Not yet. The children are separating, though."

"I see her," Shannon said.

My heartbeat thundered in my chest. I hadn't slept, but I wasn't tired, fueled by adrenaline and a bagel someone had offered me at some point in the morning.

I couldn't see the girl yet from my vantage point inside the car, but I did see the black van drive by.

The van stopped. A man climbed out and walked around to the rear of the vehicle. He opened one of the two back doors.

Now I could see the girl walking in his direction. A group of kids passed him. Even if she screamed, by the time they looked around, she'd be inside the van. So many people driving by, but all of them in a hurry. If we hadn't been here, would anyone have witnessed her abduction?

"Go, go, go!" Shannon shouted. He bolted from the garage.

I jumped from the car to see him running across the driveway and flying into Truman Grendel. Grendel staggered back and then lashed out at Shannon, connecting with his jaw before trying to run. Shannon grabbed him and threw him against the side of the van, punching him hard. The man collapsed to the sidewalk. Roughly, Shannon rolled him over, pushing down on his back with one knee. Shannon was cuffing Grendel by the time the three other officers hurried onto the scene.

I craned my neck to peer inside the open back door of the van. Nothing. Detective Roscoe climbed inside and emerged seconds later, shaking his head.

"Where is Trina Ball?" shouted Shannon, still on top of Grendel.

"I don't know what you're talking about, officer." Even with his face smashed into the sidewalk, Grendel managed to sound mocking.

A crowd was growing, both of school children and neighbors, and even passing cars were slowing down or stopping. Standing in the crowd was the blond girl who did look a lot like Alice. I wondered if the police would ever tell her parents the danger she'd so narrowly escaped.

Shannon rolled Grendel over. "So help me, after what you did to that little girl, I'm going to get it out of you one way or the other."

"Threatening me, officer?" Grendel said. "In front of all these innocent children?"

"We'll have to take him in," Roscoe said, a restraining hand on Shannon's shoulder.

Shannon's nostrils flared. "He's not going anywhere until he gives us something."

Leaving them to hash out the matter, I slipped around to the driver's side of the van. The front door was open, and I ran my hands over the seat, the steering wheel, and the dash. Nothing but annoyance. Until I touched the keys.

Probably the right mix now. I stared at the inert form of the girl, smiling. She was still breathing but definitely out. So maybe less of the mixture for the younger girl.

Or was she breathing? I couldn't really be sure. But it didn't matter. I wouldn't need her after today. It was time to move on.

I left the cabin, whistling and jiggling the keys in my hand. Keeping a copy of these after redoing the cabin had been a stroke of pure genius on my part. It was one of my best remodels, and with the owner's primary residence in Europe and their proclivity to use the cabin only during the ski season, it made the perfect place to hide until I put the next phase of my plan into action.

Better hurry. The food I paid cash for would arrive later this morning. Should be enough to see us clear through summer if needed.

I started the van's engine and drove away.

He drove away, but not before I glimpse the number on the house: 418. Somewhere out there was a cabin with those numbers. And Truman Grendel had been there just over an hour ago.

A hand touched my shoulder, and I jerked around to find Shannon standing there, his bottom lip bleeding where Grendel had hit him. I expected him to lecture me on contaminating evidence, but he just said, "Find anything?"

"It's Trina Ball. We have to hurry." I told him what I'd seen, hoping he'd be able to use his contacts to put the rest of the address together.

"Just a minute." He pushed past me and leaned inside the van while I bit back my impatience.

After what seem like forever, he emerged and slammed the door. "Okay, let's go."

We turned from the van, only to run into Shannon's partner.

"Uh, what's going on here?" Roscoe said.

"Got a partial address of where he might have the girl," Shannon told him.

Roscoe's eyebrows arched so high, they were in danger of flying off his face. "Oh, yeah? Let me see."

"It's nothing you can see," I said.

He smirked. "Look, I know you've got my partner on board with this psychic stuff, but all this"—he waved his hands at the van—"is because that boy Caleb and the neighbor identified the suspect and his car in the neighborhood."

"From a drawing Ms. Rain created," Shannon reminded him.

"Fine. Play it your way, you go ahead and do whatever you feel you have to. I'll get this creep booked and interrogated. We got enough to hold him. Forensics might be able to tell us where the van's been."

Shannon didn't point out that the forensics teams were still busy at the house, but I could see it in his eyes. Then again, I didn't know him that well, so maybe I was putting my own feelings into it. I didn't much like his partner, but he seemed like a good cop.

"I'll let you know what we find," Shannon said.

"I won't hold my breath." Roscoe stalked away.

Shannon and I began the walk to the next block where we'd left his car. "So," I said, "how are we going to find the rest of the address?"

"There can't be too many cabins with that address in an hour radius. I'll have them run it for us at the station."

"You have a little blood . . . uh, here." I pointed to my own lip to show him where.

He wiped it away with a finger. "A scratch. The creep hits like a girl."

"Not like me. I took taekwondo lessons as a kid."

He laughed. "If you're going to keep reading imprints, you might want to take that up again."

"I have forgotten a lot," I admitted.

There was an easiness that hadn't been between us at any point in our relationship so far, but I knew that didn't mean he trusted me or liked what I did. He wanted to solve cases. Period.

He looked over at that moment, phone to his ear. Our

eyes caught and held. Then someone answered on the other end of the line, and he started talking.

In the end, there was only one address that matched what I'd seen, and that was in an unincorporated area of Clackamas County near a place called Rhododendron. Shannon put on his siren and we cruised along the highway so fast that I was worried about getting there in one piece. Once we turned off in Rhododendron, he barely slowed.

We came on the cabin suddenly after rounding a bend, its upscale features notable behind the thin layer of trees. "That's it." I confirmed. "But how are we going to get in?"

Shannon pulled out a set of keys. "I might have taken these from our perp's van. By the time they look for them, we'll have them back."

The cabin had an unremarkable entryway that was partially blocked by several large boxes. A laptop sat on a coffee table in the vaulted living room. Shannon started toward that, but I headed down the hallway, retracing Grendel's steps from the imprint. I steeled myself against the harsh reality that we might be too late, as we had been for little Alice.

There she was, a thin, frail figure on the huge king-sized bed, her dark hair spread out over the blue quilt under her. She was nowhere near the "big oaf" she'd been portrayed by Grendel's mind, though the points of her tiny breasts under the shirt showed the beginnings of maturation. She lay with one arm secured to the bedpost by black straps I'd forgotten seeing in the imprint, but remembered now. She didn't look as if she'd moved since Grendel had left her here.

I rushed to her side, but somehow Shannon was there in front of me. His eyelashes momentarily left shadows on his face as he checked her pulse.

"She's alive," he said grimly. "Heartbeat's faint, though. I don't think we have much time."

"Call an ambulance. You have service?"

"They'll take too long. We'll meet them." Removing a knife from his pocket, he cut off the straps, while I tucked the quilt around her.

In the car, I sat in the back, cradling Trina's head and upper body. "Keep checking to see if she's breathing," Shannon told me. "We may have to resuscitate her."

I nodded. Trina appeared to be in a coma. Had she inhaled Grendel's chloroform mixture or had he made her drink it? I rubbed her cheek. "Trina, we found you. You're okay. Hold on, honey. That man will never hurt you again. Please, hold on." I kept up the dialogue, patting her cheek, rubbing her hand. Anything to let her know she wasn't alone, that she was safe.

Shannon drove like a maniac, phone jammed to his ear as he explained the emergency to hospital staff and yelled at them to hurry. Finally, he pocketed the phone.

"They're on their way. Watch for an ambulance with lights."

I didn't reply. But after ten minutes, I said, "Shannon, I think her breathing—"

"What!" he barked, twisting his neck to glance into the back seat.

"It seems better. Maybe."

In the next moment, Trina opened her eyes. They were brown, a light brown that reminded me of fall. She sucked in a breath. "It's not a dream?"

I shook my head. "No, we're taking you home."

She sighed and shut her eyes again. For a moment, I thought it was over, but she was still breathing, and her hand clutched mine.

Forever seemed to pass until we saw the ambulance racing toward us on the freeway. We swerved to the side of the road and jumped out of the car as they did a U-turn and pulled up behind us. Then it was over all too fast, with them whisking her away to Portland.

Shannon and I stood near his car, staring at the empty highway. The weak May sun shone down on us like a promise. With my bare feet planted in the dirt by the side of the road, I felt a connection with the earth. A peace.

"She's going to be okay," he said. "We did good."

I nodded. "I hope so. Just give me a moment before we go back."

He leaned against the side of the Mustang and folded his arms. "Take all the time you need."

Chapter 8

Three days passed. Tawnia had spent the last two nights at my place after I confessed I was having trouble sleeping, even with the help of my parents' book of poetry and Winter's picture of Summer.

"How can I come to terms with not saving Alice?" I asked Tawnia Friday morning.

"If you hadn't found her, you wouldn't have saved the other girl," Tawnia reminded me. "You should go to the funeral. Isn't it today? I think you need closure."

I was pretty sure going to the funeral of someone I didn't know meant I needed my head examined.

Yet hours later, I was at the mortuary. I'd gone out for a drive and an early lunch and ended up here instead. Jake would have come with me, or Tawnia, but there hadn't been time to tell them. I slipped quietly into a seat near the back of the mortuary chapel, tucking my bare feet under my dress and hoping no one recognized me.

Instinctively, my fingers went to the bump of the tiger's

eye button in the pocket of my skirt. I'd been carrying it around since Tuesday, unsure what I was going to do with it. I wouldn't touch the button with my bare hand because of the imprint, but I couldn't bring myself to give it to the police or throw it away. It had represented hope to a little girl who had desperately needed something to help her hold on.

"Uh, excuse me," a woman behind me leaned forward to say. "They're trying to get your attention."

I looked to the front of the chapel in time to see Mr. Craigwell separate himself from his family and move in my direction. With effort, I gave myself a mental push and came to my feet, stumbling into the aisle.

Just give him your condolences, I thought.

I opened my mouth, but before anything came out, Mr. Craigwell said, "I'm glad you're here. I've been wanting to thank you."

"Thank me?" I hoped I didn't look as stunned as I felt.

"Without you . . ." The big man's voice wavered, but he plunged on. "Without you, we might never have learned the truth. We may never have found her. Or it may have been years."

I should have something comforting to say to him, but I didn't. He didn't seem to notice.

"Every day I wish it had ended differently," he continued. "God knows that I do. I've cursed God and myself and everything that went wrong that day. I've sworn to kill that sick creep." He took a deep breath. "But I also talked to the other girl's parents, and they told me a little of what their daughter suffered. I'm glad . . . I'm glad my baby didn't have to endure that. At least we have that much. We know she's at rest." He was crying now, and so was I.

I started to hug him, and he enveloped me completely with his big arms.

"I'm sorry," I whispered. Sorry that I hadn't made it in time. Sorry that nothing anyone could have done would have changed his daughter's fate.

"I know." He stepped back bringing both hands up to wipe his cheeks. "Look, you ever need anything, you come to me." With a watery smile, he released me and strode back toward his family.

I stared after him until I felt someone touching my arm. I turned to see Detective Shannon Martin standing next to me. His eyes were as beautiful as I remembered, and the rest of him also looked good in the black suit. Only the scruff on his face, which had grown past the point of ruggedness, looked rather disheveled. He was still hot, though, if anyone cared to notice.

He'd probably come to pay his respects like I had.

"He's right, you know," Shannon said in a low voice. "Apparently, Grendel was also responsible for the death of his only sister five years ago. We found her buried at a property he owns in Mexico. If not for you, he might have gotten away with killing both girls. And more."

I tried to hit a mocking tone. "So I guess you didn't come to arrest me?"

He gave me a smile that was every bit as mocking. "Not this time. You were in Kansas last week, as you said, and we've found no connection between you and Grendel."

Was he serious? He'd checked? "Just when I think you're starting to be human," I muttered, collapsing into the nearest chair.

To my annoyance, he settled next to me. "What?"

"Forget it." It was his problem, not mine.

"Anyway, we've already linked him to at least two assaults on young teens before he kidnapped Trina Ball. All of it together means they're going to seek the death penalty. Regardless, he's never getting out of prison."

"Good." I'd been against the death penalty before this week, but the utter lack of remorse in Grendel's imprints was a convincing argument for the sentence.

"You deserve credit on this case. It would be within your right to talk to the media." He jerked his head toward the woman who had spoken to me earlier. "There's a reporter right there. I'll back you up."

"No way. Keep me out of it." Reporters had already mentioned an unnamed psychic and while I could use the business in my shop, I didn't want to be part of a media circus because of my gift.

Or was it my curse?

My refusal seemed to surprise him. He let several minutes go by before picking up the conversation. "Look, I stopped by your shop this morning, but you weren't there. Your boyfriend wouldn't tell me where you went."

By boyfriend, he must mean Jake. "He didn't know."

"After the funeral, can you take a ride?"

"Don't tell me you need me to solve another case." The queasiness of my stomach belied my smirk.

"Okay, I won't." He cracked a smile. "Just come along."

"All right. But I have my car. I'll follow you."

Less than two hours later, we ended up at the hospital, where the floors felt cool and welcoming against my bare feet after the heat from the sidewalk outside. I began to suspect what Shannon intended.

"How is she?" I asked.

"She woke up yesterday. Doctors say she's going to be fine. She'll need counseling, but I've talked with the parents, and they're already on top of it."

"Good." Suddenly, more than anything in the world, I wanted to see Trina Ball awake and doing well.

Shannon paused outside a door. "Look, you should know that we have more than enough to convict Grendel a hundred times over, but we've found zero connection between him and the cabin. Whatever deal he had with the owners, he's hidden it well. They may have paid him abroad. It might have been months before we tracked his path to the cabin, if we ever did. No matter how you look at it, Trina's alive only because of you."

Before I could react, he turned into the room. Trina's room. She lay in bed, each of her hands held by a parent. "Here she is as promised," Shannon announced. "This is the woman who found Trina."

The parents jumped up and came toward me, gratitude shining in their faces. "We can never thank you enough," the mother said. "Never." The father nodded, repeating his wife's thanks. I shook their hands and mumbled words I didn't register.

"Come closer," Trina called.

I moved past the parents until I was standing near the bed.

"You were in the car," Trina said. "I was so cold. I was floating away. You called me back."

"I hope that's okay." *Back* meant dealing with what had happened to her.

She nodded, grinning through her tears. "It's okay." Her eyes sought the faces of her parents. "I'm home."

Her mother rushed back to the bed and took her daughter's hand. "We're going to be with you every step of the way."

I removed the button from my pocket and quickly dropped it on the blanket in front of Trina. "I found this. I can throw it away if you'd rather, but it seemed special. You might need it . . ." On tough days. To remind herself that she was strong.

Trina snatched up the button with her free hand, running her thumb over the rounded side. "I thought I'd lost it. Thank you for finding it—and me."

"You're welcome."

The helpless anger I'd been holding in dissipated. It hadn't been easy, but I'd used my gift to save lives.

As we said goodbye and left the room, Shannon wore a smile that seemed less mocking than his usual smirk. "What?" I said.

"It feels good, doesn't it?"

Really good, but I wasn't going to admit how much I'd needed to see this family happy. "Have you been home to sleep yet?" I asked. "You do know that you need a shave, right? I didn't think cops could have beards."

"I slept last night," he conceded. "Overslept, in fact. No time to shave."

"Aw, that explains both the beard and why you aren't as grouchy."

He blinked at that. "I prefer to think of it as driven. Look, Ms. Rain . . ." He brought a plastic bag of small items from his suitcoat pocket. "I was hoping you could check a couple objects for me. Nothing too serious, I just need to verify a hunch that a suspect is telling the truth."

I blinked. "So you do need my help."

He winced, which told me he wasn't all that happy about it himself. "It's the last time," he said.

I sincerely doubted that. We lived in the same city, after all, and he was "driven."

"Fine," I said, "but you might as well call me Autumn, because no matter what you say, I've got the feeling we'll be seeing more of each other."

In a totally platonic way, of course. Which was fine because I couldn't respect a man who didn't respect me. Besides, there was Jake.

"And you have to buy me lunch," I added. "I haven't eaten yet, and reading imprints on an empty stomach always makes me cranky."

"I've noticed," he said. "Okay, you've got yourself a deal. I even know a place I think you'll enjoy."

"Then I'll let you drive. You can bring me back here for my car later."

"Only if you promise to keep your hands off my stuff."

"Fine." I didn't want to read his stuff again—especially his steering wheel—any more than he wanted me to.

But just for that comment, I would order the most expensive thing in the restaurant. No, make that two of the most expensive thing. I deserved double.

Sneak Peek

Touch of Rain

Chapter 1

My breath came faster as I stared into the shoe box sitting on the counter at my antiques shop. None of the items inside was exceptionally valuable or remarkable in any way—a kaleidoscope of bric-a-brac and childhood keepsakes that had once made up a young woman's life.

A missing young woman.

I met Mrs. Fullmer's swollen, tear-stained eyes, small and brown inside the fine scattering of wrinkles that were evidence of her suffering. Her hands tightly gripped the edges of the box holding her daughter's possessions, though the box sat on the counter between us and needed no support.

I didn't want to do this. I didn't have to. If I refused, Jake would escort the couple quickly outside and make sure they didn't return. I was very near to fainting as it was, though more with fear of what I would discover than of what the box contained. I'd learned the hard way that some emotions left imprinted on random objects were better off undiscovered.

"You okay, Autumn?" Jake's voice was both worried and curious. He smiled tentatively, his teeth white against his brown skin.

"I'm fine," I said.

A soft snort came from Mr. Fullmer. "Maybe we should be going."

An unbeliever. I didn't blame him. I hadn't believed in psychometry myself when the imprints had begun, and I hadn't told anyone about my strange gift for months after. I'd confessed to Tawnia first, and that my practical sister believed me was a testament to the connection between us—despite our having spent the first thirty-two years of our lives apart.

Jake Ryan was the second person I'd told. Solid, reliable Jake, who was gorgeous despite—or perhaps because of— his chin-length dreadlocks, or locs as he called them. When he was at the counter in my store, women bought more of my antiques just to see him smile or to have an excuse to talk to him. He had increased the sales in the Herb Shoppe considerably since I'd sold Winter's business to him. Winter Rain, my father.

Silently, I met Mr. Fullmer's gaze and saw him notice my mismatched eyes, his mouth opening slightly in surprise. People are always surprised when they look at me long enough to actually see my eyes. I didn't give him credit for seeing, though, as we'd met already once before and because he'd been staring at me for the past five minutes, searching for obvious flaws. He took a step back, which I regarded as defeat.

"If there's any chance Victoria left a clue," Mrs. Fullmer said in her breathless voice, "we have to try. She's been gone for months."

When no one spoke further, I slowly removed the four oversized antique rings from my fingers and handed them to Jake, the comforting, pleasant buzz they gave off ceasing the moment I released them. Wearing them wouldn't prevent me from reading other imprints, but it would soften them, and I didn't want that now. I reached for an object. A hairbrush. I held it in one hand, running the fingers of my other hand over the polished length, pushing at the hair-entwined bristles.

A face in a mirror, a narrow, pretty face with long, blond hair. There was a sound at the door and a flash of an angry man staring down at me, words falling from his lips: "You are not going tonight, and that's final!" The urge to throw the brush at his face, an urge at least nine months old.

I shook my head and set the brush back in the box. I'd recognized the girl as Victoria from the picture they'd shown me and the man as Mr. Fullmer, but the scene hadn't told me anything except that once last year Victoria had been angry enough to want to throw the hairbrush at her father. She hadn't done it, though, and the memory was already fading. Mentioning it now wouldn't help them find her. I moved to the next item, passing purposefully over the new-looking socks and worn swimming suit.

I'd learned by touching everything of Winter's after

his death that distinct feelings or imprints remained intact only on belongings connected with great emotion. Objects a person treasured most or held while experiencing extreme levels of joy, fear, worry, or sadness. Items that weren't often washed or forgotten.

For Winter that meant the colorful afghan my adoptive mother, Summer, had crocheted, the first vase I'd made on my wheel when I'd gone through my pottery stage, his favorite tea mug with the sad-looking puppy on it, his plain wedding band. And of course, his cherished picture of Summer, the one I'd dropped in shock and surprise on the day of his funeral eleven months ago, causing the glass to shatter. It was the first object that had "spoken" to me.

Other objects gave off a muted sensation, a pleasant low hum, but no clear images or scenes I could relive when the burden of missing Winter became too great. I never found anything among his possessions that contained angry or hateful imprints. He must have long ago come to terms with those feelings. My adoptive father had been an exceptional man.

My hand settled on the journal from the Fullmers' box, but I could tell right away this hadn't been a real journal for the missing girl. No emotional imprints, except perhaps the barest hint of old resentment. If she'd written in the book at all, it hadn't been willingly.

I picked up the prom pictures instead. Victoria was a slim, pretty, vivacious girl, and her date equally attractive, but though he was nice enough, the girl hadn't been attracted to him. The feeling had been strong enough to leave a faint residue of distaste on the picture when she'd held it in her hands as recently as six months earlier, which would have been mid-December, several weeks before her disappearance. I set it down.

The sea shell hinted at the ebb and swell of the ocean, the girl's possession of it not long enough or felt deeply enough to make an imprint. An old compact mirror with jeweled insets radiated a soothing tingle. Most of my antiques were like that, the emotions clinging to them soft and old and comfortable. I believe that feeling is why I went into the antiques business. Perhaps the objects had quietly hummed to me all along, though I hadn't yet understood their language.

Even in the old days there had been attractive items I'd never wanted to bring to my store, and now that I was conscious of my gift, or curse as I sometimes thought of it, I suspected those were the antiques that had fresher, negative imprints, perhaps even violent ones. A cast iron statue at an estate sale last month had flashed a terrifying image of crushing a human skull. No way had I wanted that statue in my shop. I didn't care that my markup would have been phenomenal.

I let my hand glide over several more objects in the Fullmers' shoe box, scanning for emotions that might be clues for Victoria's mother. The letter (contentment long faded), the porcelain figurine of a ballet dancer (sleepy dream of the future), a book of poetry (whisper of an old crush). To tell the truth, I wasn't positive any of these weak impressions were real or if my mind showed me only what I expected to find. These items had obviously been important to the missing girl at one time, though, or she wouldn't have kept them all these years.

Not until I reached the black velvet jewelry box did I feel a jolt. My hand closed over it, my palm covering the small object completely. Even through the box, the emotion was strong—too strong to come from even my active imagination . . .

END OF SNEAK PEEK. If you would like to purchase *Touch of Rain* please visit your online bookstore to order. To learn more about the author and her books, please continue on to the About the Author page.

Other books in the Imprints series.

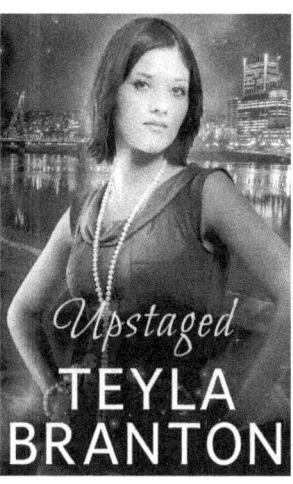

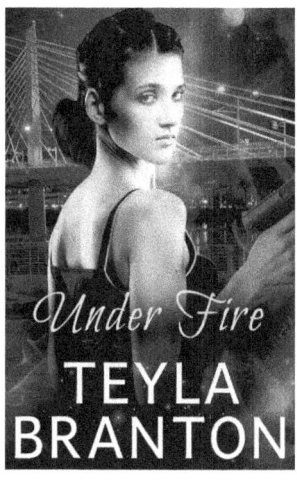

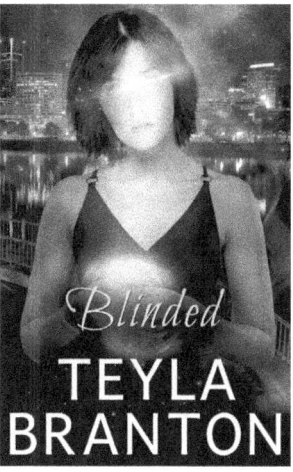

TEYLA BRANTON has worked in publishing for over twenty years. She loves writing women's fiction and traveling, and she hopes to write and travel a lot more. As a mother of seven, it's not easy to find time to write, but the semi-ordered chaos gives her a constant source of writing material. She's been known to wear pajamas all day when working on a deadline, and is often distracted enough to burn dinner. (Okay, pretty much 90% of the time.) A sign on her office door reads: Danger. Enter at Your Own Risk. Writer at Work.

Under the name Teyla Branton, she writes urban fantasy, paranormal romance, and science fiction. She also writes romance, romantic suspense, and women's fiction under the name Rachel Branton. For more information or to sign up to hear about new releases, please visit www.TeylaBranton.com.